SEASON ONE: EPISODE FIVE

SUNSET CHRONICLES

BLACK CLOUD

PAUL STEPHENSON

HOLLOW STONE

Note for readers

The Sunset Chronicles is a sci-fi serial. Think of it like a series, much like you'd get on your favourite tv streaming service. There are seasons, split up into episodes (five per season). Each episode is designed to be read in roughly two hours, though fast readers may blast through them even quicker, and those who like to really get stuck into the story may take longer. They're intended to be thrilling and exciting, and are released regularly each month so that you can keep up with the story even if you have a hectic schedule. And who doesn't, these days? It's perfect for if you want to slip some space horror into your lunch break, or if you want to binge it of an evening.

If you've come to this book first, please check out episode one, *Last Light*, which is available in print and ebook.

Also, although *The Sunset Chronicles* is a story that stretches from the ice moon of Europa to every corner of the globe, its author remains English. As such, international readers should note that spellings are of the UK variation of English, so if you see a typo, it must be because of that.

If you're in the UK and you see a typo, it must be your imagination.

For King, Wyndham, Giger, Hill, Atwood, Stoker, Shelley, Eis-
ner, Del Toro, Goddard, Jackson, Matheson, Cronin, Foster, and
all the other geniuses I can only dream of emulating.

Chapter One

Lois woke on an uncomfortable mattress, covered in dust accumulated over decades. She'd fallen drunkenly on top of it and slept in her clothes, and it took more than a few moments for her to work out where the hell she was, and why she was there.

Stumbling into the lounge, she found Kat already up and drinking coffee, the aroma almost enough to revive Lois from her walking slumber.

'Is that real coffee?' she asked in a cracked voice. She realised how bad the inside of her mouth tasted for the first time.

'It's instant, and about ten years past its sell by date, but yeah. Still tastes better than synth shit. I made you a cup. It's in the kitchen.'

'Thanks.'

'So what's the plan?' Kat asked, as Lois brought her coffee back through, breathing in its heavy fumes.

Lois sat on the sofa, trying to fight her brain through the fug of whatever the hell they'd been drinking the night before. In that fog, only one thing was simple. 'I'm going to get the hell out of Atlanta, get my family the hell out of the country.'

'Run away?'

'I don't see another option, do you?' All Lois cared about was getting Marisa and the girls and trying to find somewhere where Sunset's reach didn't extend. If there was such a thing.

Except, she knew full well there wasn't.

'Fight?' Kat said. There was a defiance in her eyes which hadn't been there the day before.

Lois sighed. 'I tried to get dirt on Sunset, and I failed. It's not like I can go back in there. If I get out of the city without having my throat cut, I'd consider that a win.'

'Your handler's death goes unpunished? And mine?' Kat asked, matter-of-factly.

The sight of Findlay's body flashed briefly in Lois's mind. Heat rose up her neck. 'Fuck you,' she said. 'There's nothing I want more that to see those bastards burn.'

Kat leaned back, shrugging. 'You say that, but you don't seem bothered about finding out what happened to him.'

'I know what happened to him,' Lois shouted, surprising herself with the volume. She took a breath and calmed her voice. Kat was baiting her, and she was allowing herself to be baited. 'I saw the body. We both know who did it.'

'But you don't know why.'

That stumped Lois. Of course, she knew the immediate why. There was something on that pad. Something bad enough to frighten the hell out of Burgess, or Carlos. Hell, the order could have come from the top, from Christopher Sun himself. But why?

If there was a way of avenging Findlay, and Sardy, and Kat's handler, it was that. Find out what they were so scared of, take it public. There were still a few days before the contract for Sunset's takeover of law enforcement went through. How satisfying would it be to spoil that party?

On the flip side to that argument sat Marisa and the girls. Exposed. Vulnerable. Sunset could reach out and grab them easily. It would take Sunset Security five minutes to work out they'd gone to Lois's parents, and there was nobody there to protect any of them. She was alone, except for the family she could run to, and the agent sat across from her.

And yet, where would running get them? A life looking over her shoulder, likely a short one, at that. They'd never be free. The only freedom she could gain for herself, for her family, was to win. And win big.

She sighed. 'The chip. It's the only leverage, and it's in one of three places. If there's an answer, it's on there.'

Kat leaned forward, a smile on her face. 'Okay. What are the options?'

'Option one, it's embedded in the door frame to my house, which is doubtless under Sunset surveillance. That's the best-case scenario. Option two, it's at Findlay's apartment, where there are cops, and which is also doubtless under Sunset surveillance. If that's the case, it'll be near impossible to find. I know Findlay, and he could hide an elephant in a swimming pool and not have anyone know it's there. If the chip is there, it might as well have washed out to sea.'

'What's option three?'

'Sunset already have it, and it's locked up tight.'

'If that were true, they wouldn't be turning you into America's public enemy number one,' Stone said, picking up a decade old pad. Lois's face, emblazoned on the news feed, a picture completely unfamiliar, like a mugshot never taken.

'Is that...'

'National feed. There's no running and hiding from this.'

Lois stared at the tiny screen. Marisa would see this. Her parents would. Across the country—across the world—every criminal she'd ever burned. Every woman she'd shared a bed with.

The floor seemed to sink underneath her, swallowing her whole, except she never moved. She stared at the screen.

'So,' Stone said. 'What say we go check out your house first?'

Chapter Two

She'd been on hundreds of stakeouts in her years as an investigator, but Lois never thought she'd be staking out her own empty house. There it stood, anonymous in its Atlantan genericness. On the plus side, Sunset hadn't turned it over. No windows smashed, and the door remained intact. On the outside, at least, all was calm.

They were less than a hundred metres away, in a house across the street. Mrs Pinkerton's house, in fact. Lois knew where she kept her spare key, and that the old spinster would be out at her club for the day. It was what the old woman lived for—that and gossip. She'd be down there prattling on about her nationally renowned neighbour, the one she'd always known was a wrong'un, leaving her family alone for months at a time.

Let her have her gossip, Lois thought. I'll take her home for a few hours.

Her blonde hair was brown now, cut short courtesy of a quick butchering by Kat, who'd also sourced new clothes for the pair of them. The Detective wasn't burned yet apparently, although she wasn't willing to risk walking into the police precinct to test the theory. Lois didn't blame her.

Kat sat beside her in the old woman's bedroom, watching for signs of the surveillance Sunset had to have set up. They sat in silence, watching the rooftops, looking for curtain twitches while trying not to twitch their own.

'I don't suppose those scopes can tell if there's a chip still embedded in the door frame?' Lois asked.

'Take a look,' Kat replied, handing them over. 'You know where you left it.'

Lois zoomed in, but it wasn't powerful enough. One of them would have to go to the door.

A curtain twitched.

'Shit,' Lois said.

'You see someone?'

'Curtain.'

'Which one.'

Lois backed away from the window. 'Mine.'

'I'm pretty sure you're not home.'

'Yeah.'

Sunset security were in her house. Or Atlanta PD. Either way, it felt pretty grim to know people were in there, amongst her things. Amongst Marisa's and the children's things. The twitching curtain was her bedroom, which added to the crawling sensation across her skin.

'How do we get close enough to check?' Kat asked.

'I don't see we can,' Lois replied.

'It might help if we knew who was in there.'

'How?'

'If it's local PD I could go in, hope I'm not burned, distract them long enough for you to go to the door and check.'

'That's a hell of a risk.'

'I don't have a better idea.'

'What if it's Sunset?'

'It'll get interesting.'

Five minutes later, Kat wandered across the street. Lois watched from the safety of her neighbour's house. Kat reached Lois's front door and knocked. Nobody answered, as expected. If people lay in wait, they were hardly going to answer the door. Kat made a show of going to the downstairs window, peering through them. Seeing nothing, she went round the back.

Lois took her cue and left the neighbour's house, hood pulled up over her head, sunglasses masking her eyes. She crossed the road trying to hide her usual gait, a task made easier by the limp carried from the previous day's escape.

Resisting the urge to look up at the windows as she went past her house, she stopped past it, leaning against the wall of the next house along, careful not to trample the plastic plants.

She waited.

A loud crash came from inside her house, and a muffled gunshot. Not quite the plan, but here was her window. Never mind what was happening inside. Walking back to the front door, her fingers moved along the wooden frame, trying to find the place where the chip sat. It wasn't there. She double checked, knowing full well it was pointless. The chip was gone, along with any hope they might have.

Stepping back from the door, she tried to ignore the violence going on over the other side and think. If Findlay got the chip before his death, he'd have replaced it with a fresh chip for the following day, but there wasn't one.

Sunset had it.

Another crash from inside. It didn't sound like an amicable conversation, a scream from Kat confirming it.

Without thinking, Lois placed her palm against the lock and burst in through the front door.

In the hallway, Kat struggled with three agents grappled onto her in an attempt to bring her down. The man holding her throat from behind had lost his black mask; blood smeared his face. Two others gripped onto the swinging limbs Kat tried to fight them off with.

Lois picked up a ceramic vase given by Marisa's grandmother as a wedding present shortly before passing away. It was one of the few pieces still standing in a house resolutely trashed. Before the men could take in her appearance, she crossed the distance, swinging the vase at the man holding Kat's neck.

The vase connected with the side of his head, shattering it into shards of pottery. He crumpled, dragging Kat to the floor with him. Before Lois could congratulate herself, a guard gave her a swift punch to the ribs, slamming her into the wall. A second fist swung toward her, connecting with her ear before she could move out of its way. She fell to her knees in pain, her ears ringing.

Thankfully, Kat was already back on her feet, chopping the throat of one man with her palm before following it up with a kick to the balls of the other. Both stumbled back, clutching their respective pain, unable to block the follow up punches sending them to the floor, unconscious.

The man Lois hit with the vase got to his feet, looming over Lois as she tried to get up. Lois kicked up at his face as hard as she could, but missed by a distance. He smirked, until she landed the second attempt squarely between his legs. He fell back to the floor. This time he didn't get back up.

'Thanks,' Kat said, breathlessly. 'But weren't you supposed to get the hell out of here?'

'No chip. No replacement, either. I guess Sunset has it already.'

Kat put her hands on her knees, bent over, trying to regain her breath. All she could offer in response was a nod.

'You okay?' Lois asked.

'Winded. I'll be fine. They knew who I was when I came through the door. I guess word's out.'

'What now?'

Kat motioned to the unconscious men. 'Wake one of them up and find out what they know.'

'I'll get some rope,' Lois said.

Chapter Three

'Don't move,' Wyn said. She made a slow circle, checking for escape routes, but the creatures surrounded them.

'Wasn't planning on it,' Barnes replied.

Both the flamethrower and the bolt gun lay on the ground a few feet away, discarded in a moment of carelessness.

A loud bark sounded out across the animals. It reminded Wyn of the sounds the Sea Lions made when Mama and Baba took her to the Sea Life centre, trying to cheer her up as she settled into her new African life. She'd loved the Sea Lions, loved watching them performing for their human masters, right up to where they made a splash, soaking Wyn in a thick wave of blue water. Wyn screamed and screamed, Baba trying to convey to the worried park rangers why she wouldn't stop.

But these weren't sea lions, and Wyn couldn't scream until Baba took her home.

One creature inched forward, sliding on its front, claws digging into the ice. It sniffed the air, and when it was a few feet away from them, it tapped the ground with its domed head bone.

'Sonar,' Zoe said, sitting up, coming round. 'Of sorts, anyway.'

Wyn tried to keep still, despite every instinct telling her to get the fuck out of there, to run, sprint, leave the others to be food. Climb back in her rocket ship and fly, far, far away from here. Her breath caught in her throat as the creature drew close.

It sniffed the air and tapped the ice once more with its head. Wyn could see every scar on the creature's face. Its milky white eyes darted about, not seeming to see them. It dilated its nostrils, sniffing at the air.

There was no pigment; the only variants to its pure white were the dull grey of its scars and red remnants of its algae diet.

It stood, revealing its full size, nearly double Wyn's height. She shuddered as it expanded its nostrils once more, letting loose a horrible sucking sound. A slow hiss emanated from its mouth, which widened to reveal closely knitted, serrated teeth.

Beads of sweat formed on Wyn's forehead. She tried to keep ragged breaths from turning into hyperventilation. If it lashed out, there was nothing she could do except jump out of its way, let the lack of gravity carry her away. Even that was a long shot. If it attacked, she'd be dead in a second.

At least it'd be quick.

'We come in peace,' she shouted.

'Really?' Barnes muttered 'That's what we're going with?'

She couldn't tell if the creature could hear her through the helmet, but it froze. It sniffed the air again, backing up. It gave a bark, loud enough to rattle the fillings in Wyn's teeth, and turned away.

Another bark followed, further away this time. No, not one bark—several—a choir of tuneless barking. As one, the creatures moved around the three of them, falling to their stomachs and propelling themselves across the ice at great speed. They circled once, broke, and headed away in a line.

The three of them were alone again.

'Jesus fucking wept,' Barnes said, his voice shaking. 'I can't believe that worked.'

'It was that or we're here for your poop,' Wyn replied.

'They were sussing us out,' Zoe said. 'They're not going to be a threat if they don't think we are.'

'Hey, Zo, how are you feeling?' Wyn said, rushing to the dazed biologist.

'I don't know,' she replied, coughing. 'What the hell did you give me, doc?'

'A magician never reveals his secrets,' Barnes said, helping Zoe to her feet, taking the weight of her bandaged side. 'No, don't stand on it.'

'Where the hell are we?' Zoe asked, looking around at the nothing surrounding them.

'There's a problem,' Wyn said. 'But no time to think about it. We've got to find the others.'

'Find them?' Zoe asked.

'That's the problem,' Wyn said. 'We got sent in the wrong direction.'

'What?' Zoe and Barnes said in unison.

'If we don't haul arse, it won't matter.'

They walked as briskly as possible, following the path laid out by Miles, their way made easier by Zoe's transformation from dead weight to semi-functioning person. She winced with every step, but the lack of gravity helped keep the weight off her injured side.

'Ship's computer intentionally took us off course, steered us in the wrong direction.' Wyn said once they got a steady rhythm going.

'Fucking AI, man,' Barnes said.

'It wasn't Miles,' Wyn said. 'Miles saved us, he sneaked communication across to your pad.'

'Great,' Barnes said. 'Betrayed by one piece of technology, saved by another. How do we know Miles isn't steering us wrong?'

'Got a better idea?' Wyn asked.

'I'm serious,' Barnes said. 'Ship's computer isn't a sentient piece of software, Wyn. There's no way it could decide to send us in the wrong direction. Only Miles could do that.'

'You're assuming this was a deliberate mistake,' Zoe said. 'It could be ship's computer glitched or miscalculated.'

'Or it was Hamza's pet,' Barnes said.

'There is another option,' Wyn said. 'Someone didn't want us to make it.'

'Why the hell would they want that?' Barnes asked, incredulous.

Wyn stopped squaring up to the doctor. 'Don't you think you're being paranoid about Miles?'

'Guys,' Zoe said.

'Oh yeah, because there's no history of AI programs glitching out on their creators, is there?'

'Guys!' Zoe said, pointing across the ice.

The lights of the mining operation glowed on the horizon.

'Thank fuck,' Barnes said.

'Think you might owe someone an apology,' Wyn muttered. 'Come on, we still need to haul arse if we're going to make it.'

They started across the ice again, Wyn turning the lights on her helmet to full blast to alert the crew. As they grew closer, it became clear they had competition for their attention.

Hundreds of the creatures hurtled past the rest of the crew—seemingly oblivious to the surrounding equipment—toward the fissure in the ice.

'Is that...' Barnes asked.

The creatures ran at the fissure, head first, before disappearing.

'Ha!' Zoe exclaimed. 'That's what the domed heads are for. They're going under the ice, too.'

'What the hell?' Wyn asked.

'They can't survive the magnetotail,' Barnes said.

The crew ahead seemed torn between trying to finish their work and staring at the creatures running around them.

Wyn trudged on, Barnes and Zoe following a few paces behind. Wyn's visor counted down. Thirteen minutes.

A herd of galloping creatures whisked past them at pace, narrowly missing the three of them. It'd be just their luck to get caught in a stampede a hundred metres from the others.

They crossed the distance at a dash, the rest of the crew not noticing their arrival until they were a few metres away.

'You made it!' Captain Davis said, grasping Wyn tightly. The rest of the crew were too busy. Stef fussed with a huge contraption stood atop the ice that looked for the world like the most incongruous door in history. Ermine hooked up a long pipe to the tracker, which bore an enormous tank atop it to store any samples they gleaned under the surface. Hamza backed the tracker up.

'Just about,' Wyn said, taking in the scene. 'How are we doing?'

'We're there,' Stef said, stepping back from her work to admire it. 'Hey Wyn. Good to see you.'

'How's Zoe?' Captain Davis asked.

'Well, I'm here,' Zoe said. She looked exhausted.

'What took you so long?' Ermine asked.

'Let's worry about it later,' Stef said. 'We need to get under the ice, pronto.'

'Li's down already. Stef, you're up next.'

'He get down okay?' Wyn asked, eyeing the tubing suspiciously.

'We'll find out soon enough,' Stef said.

'Tube came back empty,' Captain said. 'That's good enough.'

Stef stepped forward and opened up the door. Inside the grandiose frame was a thin metal tube. Stef stepped in, pulled the door closed on herself, and disappeared in a flash. Wyn gasped.

'Ermine, you're up.'

Ermine stepped forward and repeated the process. This time Wyn watched more closely, wishing she'd paid more attention to their briefings.

Ermine stepped in and closed the door. A light on the door changed from green to red. The surrounding chamber filled with water, and Ermine shot down. The light turned green again, and the chamber emptied of water. All in the blink of an eye.

'Barnes,' the Captain said.

'You sure?' Barnes said. 'Doesn't look much fun to me.'

'Get in there, Barnes, or we die.'

'Fine,' Barnes said. He stepped in, and he too was gone.

'Do we know if this is even working?' Wyn asked again.

The Captain shook his head. 'No, they haven't established communication lines down there yet.'

'So we're hoping...'

'We're not about to plummet to our deaths? Pretty much.'

Wyn took a deep breath and watched Hamza disappear. Zoe went next, her face white as a sheet. God knew what the trip would do to her wound, or the patch Wyn had fashioned in her suit.

If they'd come in on their regular descent, they'd have had hours more to make sure everything was in place. They could have worked on a way to get Zoe under the ice safely.

Zoe's eyes filled with panic, mirrored in the flutter of Wyn's heartbeat.

Every fibre of Wyn's being screamed not to go through that door. Every time she thought about it, she got flashbacks of a London street. Of the flood.

Of a small hand slipping out of her own.

'Wyn,' Captain Davis said. 'You're up.'

Wyn took a last glance at the pad. Less than two minutes until they were in the magnetotail's wake.

She moved forward to the tube and pulled the door open, her hand trembling.

Stepping inside, she turned to face the outside. The creatures moved with a frenzied intensity, clawing over each other to get under the ice. They didn't seem too interested in the Captain or the equipment.

Wyn closed her eyes.

'You okay, Wyn?' the Captain asked. 'Your vitals are spiking.'

'Fine,' Wyn lied.

The chamber filled with water, not gradually but violently, urgently. Wyn floated up momentarily, banging the top of her helmet on the roof of the tube.

A noise worked its way out of her throat, unbidden. She fought the urge to reach out, claw at the thick tubing, reach for the door, get the hell out of there. She didn't want to—couldn't—do this.

Forcing her eyes shut, she waited. For a second, she was back on a Croydon street, a little girl with braids in her hair and her brother's tiny hand in her own. Everyone on the street rushed about, panicking, but she was too young to understand.

When the water trickled down the pavement, she opened their door to watch.

They wanted to see the water. As it rose, Tiwa splashed about in welly boots with dinosaurs on, giggling. Wyn told him they'd go inside when it got to their ankles.

Inside the house, Mum rushed about the kitchen, gathering what she could move to the upper floors. Baba took carvings from the wall, throwing them roughly into a box. Wyn's job was to watch her brother.

In the tube, the light turned from red to green, and the bottom fell out of Wyn's world.

Out in the street, Wyn watched the family across the road run to their car. Silly. Even Wyn knew the news said there was no point trying to use the roads. They should get to higher ground. Wyn and Tiwa would be safe in their bedrooms. Wyn didn't understand what the fuss was about, anyway. It was a game to her, and to little Tiwa. A year between them.

Tiwa.

His beautiful face. His big brown eyes. His wide smile as his boots splashed in the puddle.

The wave came from nowhere, yet seemed to swell from everywhere. As high as the houses on either side of the street. Wyn saw it, but too late.

A scream came from behind—her mother's. Wyn reached out. Grabbed her brother's hand. Fingers closed around his. The panic in his eyes as the water hit. His hand wrenched from her own.

He was gone. Her mother, screaming.

Screams filled her ears as Wyn fell through the ice, plummeting to the Gods knew what fate.

Chapter Four

'Mmmm, mmm fff.' The man said, somewhat uselessly.

'We'll let you know when we're ready to hear what you've got to say,' Kat said, patting his knee.

Their interrogee sat tied to one of Lois's kitchen table chairs, secured by old ropes last used to move the refrigerator in. They stuffed his mouth with a dishrag from the sink. Lois wasn't sure how clean it would be, but that was tough shit.

Lois pulled up two chairs opposite him; they each took one, staring at the man. His eyes filled with panic.

'Don't worry,' Lois said. 'You give us the answers we want; we won't have to kick you in the balls again.'

He fixed them with a stare; the hardened look of someone who's realised what their silence may cost them and decided to keep it, anyway. Usually she saw it on the face of a suspect who'd decided jail was easier to deal with than the wrath of their bosses, but she was curious to see what the threat of actual violence would do to that calculus.

'Now,' Stone said, leaning forward. 'I'm going to take this off. If you scream and holler, I will shoot you in the fucking head. I've got two more chumps I can tie up and ask questions. Okay?'

The man hesitated before nodding. Stone removed the dishrag, and the man coughed.

'You work for Sunset Secure, right?' Lois asked.

'I'm not telling you anything,' he replied.

'Dude, you're wearing a Sunset Secure uniform. You can confirm that much to us.'

He said nothing.

'Where's the chip?' Lois asked.

The man made no response, but his eyes flickered, ever so briefly, to the unconscious and trussed body of his fallen comrade. Lois fought the urge to get up and check—no need to let him know he'd given the game away.

'Don't know what you're talking about,' he lied.

'Let me guess,' Stone said, patting him on the knee. 'You're a grunt, wouldn't know shit, go where they tell you, right?'

'Yeah.'

'Then you're no fucking use to us,' Stone replied, getting to her feet and pulling the pistol out of her waistband. She pointed it at his head and for a second Lois thought she might genuinely dash the man's brains over her dining room wall.

'Wait!' the man said, evidently buying Stone's play as much as Lois. 'We have orders. Find a chip, take you into custody and back to HQ if you showed up. I don't know anything else, please.'

'Only three of you?'

'They said they didn't think you'd come here. Something about another mission to retrieve the family.'

'Whose family?' Lois asked, standing, already knowing the answer.

'Yours,' the man said. 'Listen, I'm sorry, I am, but...'

Kat cut him off with a pistol whip, knocking him unconscious.

'Fuck,' Lois said, pacing around her living room. 'Marisa. I need to go to them.'

'You'll walk right into their trap. We don't have the chip. You'll need to barter for them. Doesn't sound like they found it.'

'They did,' Lois replied. 'Check him. I need to contact Marisa. There's still time.'

Kat patted down the guard, trying to find the chip. She stopped when she realised Lois's intentions.

'What are you doing?'

'I have to warn Marisa,' Lois replied.

'No. They don't know we've been here, don't know we've got this...'—she pulled the chip out of the man's breast pocket. 'We need to find somewhere secure to call.'

'Where the hell are we going to do that?' Lois asked. 'Sunset own the feeds.'

'I might have an idea,' Kat replied, getting to her feet, holding out the chip for Lois.

Chapter Five

'No answer,' Lois said. They stood together at one of the retro-booths dotting the campus of Morehouse College. One of the few buildings in Atlanta pre-dating the great rebuild. It looked like something out of the pages of a novel, its red brick buildings a distant echo of another age. In the years she'd been in the city, Lois hadn't even known it existed—Atlanta was a city so achingly modern and sterile it seemed half impossible this still existed.

The retro-booths were another relic of a bygone era. When Oc's first came on the scene, academic institutes banned them as both a corrosive distraction for young people, and an un-policeable way to cheat the system. As a compromise to the students—stranded far from the technologies they'd grown up with—they put in these booths. Free-standing, they afforded total privacy to whoever went into them. A safe place, free from intrusion.

Once the cops realised The League were recruiting the best and the brightest from a hundred different universities through the booths, the protections offered by the supreme court were removed. These were some of the last privacy protections to have survived the long hard road through the data war; the government, through their outsourced surveillance corps, could now eavesdrop on them freely.

Still, better than nothing, and unlikely to be monitored close enough to...

'Lois,' a voice said from within the booth.

Lois spun round, trying to work out which section of the display was active, until she came face to face with it.

With Burgess.

She sat in Lois's father's house. On his sofa. Next to Marisa.

Her wife sat at the edge of her seat, hands bound, a strip of cloth stuffed in her mouth. Two guards stood on either side, armed and clad in black. Lois couldn't see their faces, but Marisa eyed them warily.

Where were the girls?

'Marisa,' Lois called out, and her wife's attention snapped to, her eyes widening as she saw Lois. Shaking her head, she tried to talk. Nothing came through the gag.

'Hush,' Burgess said, pulling the camera back round to herself.

Lois expanded the view screen—it was as though she were there in the room with them. Marisa looked so scared.

'Now,' Burgess said, addressing Lois. 'Let's bring an end to this nonsense, shall we? Come back to the office and we can reunite you with your delightful family.'

'You let them go,' Lois said. 'I am an agent of Interpol, and this contravenes...'

Burgess's hollow laugh cut her off. 'I'm sorry, are you trying to arrest me, over the phone? What cards do you think you hold? You have no proof of wrongdoing, no evidence. Even this call doesn't exist. Come in. We can talk about how you can get yourself out of this.'

Beside her, Marisa shook her head, the movement barely perceptible.

'You let my family go,' Lois seethed, 'and I'll forget about this when it comes time to put the whole bloody lot of you in front of a tribunal.'

'Oh, Lois. Dear Lois. I don't think you understand what you're up against here.'

She nodded to the guard closest to Marisa. He stepped forward and placed the barrel of his gun to Marisa's temple.

'No, wait,' Lois started, the bravado gone from her voice. 'I have the chip.' She fished it out of her pocket and held it up to the camera. Burgess's already tight lips tightened further.

Outside the booth, Kat hammered on the door.

'I don't think you're sufficiently motivated,' Burgess said.

The soldier pulled the trigger.

Lois screamed, a howl of pain and anger filling the booth. Marisa's body slumped to the side, sliding lifelessly off the sofa onto the floor.

'Remember,' Burgess said, leaning forward, voice barely audible over Lois's grief. 'We still have your girls. Bring the chip to me, and I'll let them live.'

The feed cut out, plunging the booth into darkness.

'No!' Lois shouted, desperately trying to find something to reconnect the line. Bile rose in her throat. Her legs went from underneath her.

The door to the booth cracked open, Kat's hands reaching in. Lois was on the floor, unsure how she'd got there, struggling to control her breathing.

It was over.

Everything was over.

Chapter Six

Another week passed. At least, that's what it felt like. After a while it was hard to differentiate the days. Judd stopped looking at feeds when he was alone, preferring to stare into space. He would rage about his situation but try to use the opportunity to work on controlling his temper, usually with little to show for it but added frustration.

Walker and Mrs Smith worried about him. He could tell. Gone was their patient bedside manner. Both could barely hide their frustration at his lack of progress, but both were terrified of pushing him too far. This was his problem—they wanted him to control his gift, but he couldn't practice on anyone. As soon as the light grew within him they would back off, terrified of being stripped of the defining part of their lives. It was frustrating for them, and him. They ended at an impasse at every session, neither side willing to put so much on the table they might lose it all.

There was something else. Judd got the definite sense he wasn't the only thing on their minds. Something was going on here at the base, and they were clearly trying to keep it from him.

It started a few days ago. Walker stopped coming entirely, and Lan started running more defences against Judd's thoughts than she'd done before. There was something on their minds they didn't want him to see.

Not that it mattered to Judd. He didn't care what any of them were up to. He just wanted to leave, but he wasn't sure that would ever be on the cards. If he was the only weapon against the teeps, why would they let him loose on the world?

Lan refused to do exercises with him. Her tolerance of him dropped, and most of their sessions were her telling him information while staring out the window of Walker's study, which opened out onto the rolling hills beyond. It was the one window which never opened out onto the actual teeps who wanted him dead.

Which is where Judd found himself—half paying attention to Lan as she recounted the role of another legendary teep. This one was a woman called Agent Nine. She had infiltrated a senate intelligence briefing about the telepath menace and turned every member against a bill to introduce teep registration. Lan faced away, looking out the window, her voice so even-toned he drifted off.

'You son of a bitch,' she hissed.

His eyes snapped open. 'What?'

'I have to come here and teach you this. I'd rather be anywhere else, with anyone else, and you can't even pay me the courtesy of staying awake?'

He sat, stunned. It was the first time she'd spoken to him, actually to him, since the cafeteria.

'What do you expect, Lan?' he said. Not angry, but tired, beaten. 'Do you think I had any idea what was going to happen? That I sat and thought hey this guy is being mean; I should wipe his brain? Come on.'

They sat in silence for a moment. Still, she hadn't run for the door. A definite improvement.

'Let me ask you a question,' he asked. 'When did you know, about your gift?'

She stared back out of the window. 'I was thirteen.'

'How many times did you lose control before you learned how to use it?'

'When I lost control, shit floated around me like there was a ghost in the room. I'd shut down. I didn't wipe the gift from someone else's mind.'

'I had no idea I could. You spent the entire day with me. Did I show any signs of being a danger to you, or to anyone else? I'm sorry. The guy was a jerk, but didn't deserve what I did. I have to live with that.'

'The jerk was my boyfriend,' she said in a quiet voice. 'He's still in the hospital ward. And Agent Nine? That was my mom. The feds captured her and tortured her for information. They called her a Chinese spy. So, it pisses me off when you fall asleep in the middle of me telling you about her.'

'Shit, Lan. I'm sorry. I'm batting O for a hundred, aren't I?'

She snorted and sat down on the desk. 'I know you didn't mean to hurt him. On some level, everyone knows that. But it doesn't change what happened in that cafeteria. It scared everyone on this campus.' She reached forward and patted his hand. 'Give me time, will you?'

'Sure,' Judd said. 'Wait, did you say he was your boyfriend?'

She laughed and gave him a look.

Somewhere outside, a scream sounded, a shrill, high pierce through the calm. Both of them stared at the door to Walker's apartment.

In Judd's head, loud, clear, a word came through, not as a sound but as an image.

RED

'Shit,' Lan said, grading her jacket. She turned to Judd. 'Stay here, okay. Don't move.' She pulled open the door and headed into the corridor, leaving Judd staring at a closed door.

Chapter Seven

'Got to go,' Kat said, pulling Lois up. 'Whatever happened, you don't want to be thinking about it in the back of a Sunset glide.'

Lois nodded without understanding the words. Nothing made sense. She couldn't compute Marisa's brains splashed over the sofa her parents argued over. Mum hated the fabric, Dad begrudged paying an extra few hundred credits for the one she wanted. Now the cheap wool was soaked with Marisa's blood.

They ran. Rather, Kat ran. Lois was dimly aware of her feet moving one in front of the other, but couldn't focus through her tears to see the road. She didn't much care, either, until she remembered her girls.

It hit her like a cartoon anvil; the world crashing back into focus. They were still on campus, running. Kat alongside her. Lois didn't see anyone chasing, but they must be there.

'In here,' Kat said, pulling Lois through an old door into a long corridor. They stood panting, Lois staring at the cracked paving stones lining the floor. 'What the hell happened?' Kat asked.

'They killed her, right in front of me.'

'Who?'

'Marisa. And they have my girls.'

'Shit.'

'I have to turn myself in,' Lois said. 'Give them the chip.'

'You do that, you're all as good as dead. Me too.'

'What other option do I have?'

'Go public. We've got the chip. What the hell is on there, anyway?'

Lois leaned against the wall, legs going out from under her. Sliding down, the coarse paint scraped her back. Good. She wanted the pain.

'Lois,' Kat said, grabbing her by the shoulders. 'Stay with me, for fuck's sake. What is on this thing?'

'I don't know,' she said. 'I had a rack pad. I filmed everything I saw on it. But I saw nothing...'

She stared at the ground. A tendril of thought flapped in the breeze of her mind.

'What?'

'There was a photo. Nine people at a party. Sun, Carlos, Burgess, four Chinese military, and two of the crew of the Minos.'

'Why the hell would they care if you saw a photo of a party? When was it taken, before the Minos took off?'

'A few days before. Sunset bankrolled the mission, right? So it's hardly surprising they'd have access to the crew.'

'But there were only a few of them in the photo?'

'Ermine and the Captain. Maybe the rest of the crew were there too, out of frame. Even if not, it'd make sense to have the commanders there, right?'

Kat shook her head, brow creased in thought. 'If that's all you had, none of this makes sense. Going public with a photo of a damn barbecue won't get anyone off our backs. Unless...'

'Unless the photo itself is proof of something.'

'You've got to go back,' Kat said.

Lois stared at Kat. 'What? No. I'm surrendering.'

Stone shook her head. 'The way you get your family back is to see this through.'

'Going back into Sunset, it's suicide. Do you know what the security is like there?'

'I've spent the last year working inside Atlanta PD, which is essentially glorified secret police for Sunset. This isn't a city, it's a cult. The whole fucking city is a death trap. But we both knew that. We've worked here. You worked in the damn building. You can do this.'

Lois walked to the window. Kat was right. Submission would get her girls killed. The huge spires of Sunset HQ gleamed in the light of a dying day. 'Okay,' she said. 'How do we do it?'

Chapter Eight

Moving back through to the bedroom, Judd leaned against the frame and watched the door. He'd heard no heavy bolt engage when Lan ran out. There was nothing stopping him from walking out.

A scream sounded, somewhere far down the corridor. The lights above flickered. What the hell was going on out there? He tried to reach out with his thoughts, like they taught, but there were only whispers, like curls of smoke he couldn't grasp. He held back, not wanting to accidentally wipe anyone.

Someone ran past, displacing the tendrils of thought, and Judd was back alone in the room again. He stared at the door. Walker's words weighed heavy on his mind. What if he went out there and someone attacked him? Was he strong enough, was his gift developed enough to defend himself? Could he do so without breaking the person attacking him?

Lan might have left the door unlocked on purpose. This could be a ploy. What if someone was waiting to shred his mind? He tried to put himself in their shoes, locked up in the same facility as the only person in the entire world who could rob you of your superpower. If the roles were reversed, Judd would probably be part of the mob out to get the guy, too.

Fuck it.

He crossed to the door and tried the handle. It opened. He peered through the crack. Nobody waited for him outside, so he edged the crack wider; enough to pop his head through. The corridor outside was empty. This was the first floor of the building, and the other side of the corridor had windows overlooking the courtyard. Judd slipped out into the corridor and moved to the window, careful to stay out of sight of the courtyard itself.

He needn't have worried—everyone was too preoccupied to pay attention to him. Hundreds of blue-uniformed students ran about, gathering into groups, looking bewildered.

A glide descended, big enough to fill the courtyard. It let down retractable ladders and people surged forward to grab them and climb up. They seemed in a hurry to get out of there. The glide filled up and took off, leaving a handful behind.

Those who remained were less panicked, barking orders at others, ordering the support staff into groups. Another glide came over the top of the facility, picked up the staff, and took off.

They were leaving him behind.

It could be a hit on him, and they wanted to get everyone out in case he went nuclear. Which would at least mean they thought he could?

Footsteps sounded further down the corridor. He slipped back across the hall, easing back into Walker's room. Three uniforms hurried past.

'Down here somewhere,' one of them, a woman, barked.

'We need to get the fuck out of here,' a man replied. A third voice joined them, but they were already too far away for Judd to hear.

Slipping into the corridor, he followed. He peered round the next corner. Another empty corridor. He was about to turn back when another open door caught his eye. It opened a crack, and for a second a pair of eyes peered through.

A child's eyes.

He moved on tippy toes across to the door, pushing the door open to look inside. It was a huge dorm, rows of white beds and nothing else. Each bed was made, with little to no evidence of occupation. No pictures, no mess. The sole sign of occupation was the mass of children huddled together in the centre of the room.

Terrified, shivering, they looked at Judd with wide-eyed horror.

He held his hands out, palms facing them. 'I'm not here to hurt you,' he said.

His mind raced. Walker said teeps didn't present until their teens, but none of these kids looked anywhere close. He took in the general state of them. They were in a bad way—barely more than skin and bones, all wearing hospital gowns. No matter their colour, their skin looked pallid, thin. Some had patches shaved into their heads.

'Jesus,' Judd said.

'Mercy,' one kid said, a boy. At least, Judd thought he was a boy. It was hard to tell.

'I said I'm not here to hurt you,' Judd said.

'No,' the boy said. 'Mercy.' He pointed behind Judd.

Judd whirled round to find another child stood in the doorway. She wore the same hospital gown as the others, but her long hair wasn't shaved, just lank and dirty.

Her hand shot out.

Judd slid across the floor, shoes squeaking as she pushed him across the linoleum.

His hands circled wildly as he tried to keep his balance.

'Mercy, stop,' one kid said. It was another girl, younger than the others. She couldn't have been over eight. Tears welled in her eyes.

Mercy cocked her head, looking askance at Judd before raising her hand. Judd rose into the air, his eyes fixed on Mercy as he flailed about. He was about to say something, anything, to calm her down, when she clenched her fist and threw him against the wall.

Air rushed from his lungs as he slammed into the brickwork, his skull connecting a split second later. Released from Mercy's grip, he fell to the floor, hitting with enough force that something cracked, the sound turning his stomach. Blood filled his mouth and nose, running down his chin. Head swimming, he tried to get up, but everything hurt too much. He fell back down.

Across the room, Mercy strode to the other children. They cowered from her. Behind her, the door to the dormitory slammed shut.

Climbing onto a bed, she sat cross-legged, staring at the doors.

Judd tried again to sit up, with slightly more success than before. The little girl who tried to stop Mercy broke from the pack and ran over to him. Mercy watched her path, but made no move to stop her.

The girl helped Judd into a sitting position. His ribs hurt, and the side of his head felt mushy and full of pain. He put his finger to where a lump already swelled, but there was no blood.

He wheezed, trying to get his breath back. The girl stood in front of him, staring.

'Who are you?' she asked.

'Judd,' he replied.

'Crystal,' she replied.

'Thanks, Crystal.' He looked over at Mercy again, but her attention was back on the doors. 'Where are you from?'

Crystal shrugged. 'We were in a place together, but we moved here a few days ago.'

'Where was this place?'

She shrugged again. 'I'm from Spain, originally. My mama and papa are still there.'

'Well, Crystal, do you mind me asking what's going on here?'

'Mercy wanted to get out. We didn't like the last place. Mercy doesn't like it here. She says they're coming back, coming for us.'

'Who?'

'Soldiers. They didn't like it when the others took us. They're coming back for us. Mercy says she'll protect us.'

'How's she going to do that?'

'She's special.'

Judd nodded. 'I got that,' he said. 'What about you, are you special too?'

Crystal shrugged again. 'They tried to make us special,' she said, looking down at her feet.

'At the last place?'

She nodded. 'And here. They only run tests here, though. Not like they did at the last place.'

Somewhere outside, gunfire rattled. The huddled children quivered en masse, pulling themselves into a tighter ball.

Judd tried to stand. 'Let's find somewhere better to hide, eh?' he said, as Crystal's hand slipped into his.

'No,' Mercy said. 'We stay here. I can protect us.'

'I'm sure you can, Mercy,' Judd said. 'But if something happens to you, we need to find somewhere for the others to hide.'

'No,' she said. 'We stay here.'

Outside, someone rattled the door handle, but it held fast. Judd tried to summon the white light from within him, the only defence he could think of, but it was nowhere to be found.

Gunfire sounded, closer. The door rattled urgently.

'If that's the people from here, you should let them in,' Judd said, walking over to Mercy, having to clutch his ribs as he went. 'They rescued you last time, right?'

'They're no better than the others,' Mercy said, sulkily. She had an American accent.

The door crashed open. Three blue uniformed teeps burst into the room. Lan was at the centre of them, with two tall blond young men either side of her. Judd's heart sank as he realised one of them was the man whose gift he'd stripped.

'Thank God, kids,' Lan said, not even spotting Judd. She was the only one who didn't.

'What's this asshole doing here?' Bertrand shouted, his finger jabbing in Judd's direction.

'I...' Judd stammered, but nothing more came out.

'Leave him,' Lan said, getting between the two of them as Bertrand started to cross the space between them. 'We're here for the kids, right? Walker's orders.'

Bertrand backed off, but his eyes never left Judd.

'Get out,' Mercy said, and the three newcomers stood up straight, like ironing boards, their faces betraying the horror of losing control of themselves.

'Mercy,' Judd said, putting his hand on her arm.

A rush of images flashed through his mind. He pulled away, struggling to process what he'd seen. Burning. Pain. Fear. Unimaginable horrors. Blood. Screaming. It was a cacophony of horror spilling into his head, overwhelming him. Bursts of violence. Of locked rooms. Of a little girl, crying, wailing, screaming in pain.

'Mercy, please. They're here to help.'

Still, she didn't release them. Judd took a breath, the white light building from the centre of his chest. He seemed able to control its growth better than before. He let it blossom, and he let a tiny sliver of it cross to Mercy.

Lan and the others fell to their knees, released.

Mercy jumped off the bed, looking at Judd with absolute horror. 'What did you do?'

'I'm sorry,' he said. 'But we need to work together. These people are here to help you. I am, too.'

Lan rushed to the other children. 'Come on, kids, let's get you out of here.' She turned to Judd. 'If we can get them to the roof, there's a glide waiting to take them somewhere safe.'

'Lan, what the fuck is going on?' Judd asked.

Before she could answer, the door burst open once more, and a dozen armed soldiers, kitted out in full tactical gear, burst in.

Mercy screamed, and hell unleashed.

Chapter Nine

The tall spires of Sunset stood before them. They had a plan, but it seemed small against the towering edifice of glass and marble before them. Still, Lois felt oddly calm, as though the sight of her wife's murder had wiped out the part of her which felt fear. There were still two beautiful young girls left to lose, but whatever happened, Lois would get through the next few hours.

A rational part of Lois's mind knew she was in shock, her brain stopping the fear getting through. As useful as it was, it also dulled the senses she'd need to get through this. Thankfully, the nagging voice telling pointing that out couldn't get through the shock, either.

They both wore black, their hoods pulled up to cover as much of their faces as possible. They ditched the sunglasses the moment it became too dark to move about without stumbling into walls. Lois wished they still had them; acutely aware of the eyes scouring the skies.

She focused on the plan. Success depended on a blunt force of proof being available, so a blunt approach seemed the best option.

'You ready?' Kat asked.

'Not really.'

Kat nodded, staring up at the tower. 'Shit, me neither. See you on the inside.'

She disappeared into the shadows. It was strange to put so much faith in a stranger at a time like this. Yet here she was, literally putting her life into the hands of a fellow officer.

The long ramp up to the entrance was a walk she'd never taken before—this was the way a huge chunk of workers came to the building. She'd never had to pad up the steep hill, its road literally paved with good intentions. Sunset mission statements covered the brickwork—do only good, be the change, humanity forward—designed to psychologically bludgeon its workforce with corporate branding every morning as they trudged up to glittering towers, reading banalities and lies while surrounded by fellow worker bees.

There were no fellow worker bees this evening, however. She was alone, clad in black, keeping as close to the shadows as she could, not looking further than a few feet ahead.

She walked past service staff leaving the building, alongside a few of the suited bees; leaving for the evening having put in hours beyond their contract to impress a boss who probably didn't know their name.

At the top of the ramp stood the first challenge. Three security guards watched the outer door. More stood inside. This entrance had the lowest form of security to get in, merely requiring an access card—she'd swiped one from a tired-looking cleaner at the bottom of the ramp.

She still needed Kat to play her part.

Trying to keep her breath steady and her head down, she approached the gate. A look passed between two of the guards. They moved forward to intercept.

The explosion wasn't huge, but it was enough. A flash to their left, the shock wave hitting the glass front of the building, spreading cracks like tiny veins across the front. A tiny fireball climbed above the trees lining the path.

'What the fuck,' one guard said, his attention completely off Lois. Still, she stopped, knowing walking would be more suspicious. She turned to the fireball, hand shielding her eyes.

The guards ran toward the flames.

Lois walked through the door, scanning her pass and entering the main foyer. She passed the last guard, who was too busy staring through cracked glass at the commotion outside to notice her.

Keeping her head down, she tried to get her bearings. The lifts were the only way up. That presented another challenge; unlike the swipe cards to get through the front door, DNA scanners barred each floor's entry point, granting access only to parts of the building the person had a reason to be in. Without the chance to harvest the DNA of anyone who might be useful, the hope was Sunset hadn't deleted her file. Or flagged it. Hopefully, they'd not think her stupid enough to do what she was doing.

The scanner beeped and lit up green. Breathing a sigh of relief, she hit the button for the executive suites. She kept her face covered as best she could.

The ride was a short one, but the seconds bled into each other; the ride like an interminable crawl toward doom.

The lift came to a stop on the top floor. The door slid open, revealing an empty corridor. To one side sat the empty office of Carlos's officious secretary. Further along, huge and imposing, were the double doors to Carlos's office, which took up a huge swath of the floor.

Stepping into the corridor, Lois checked around the corners to make sure there was no ambush and headed toward the double doors. She opened them as quietly as she could.

The room was pitch black. Had she misjudged this? She'd assumed Carlos would be here, his legendary dedication to the role keeping him long into the night, especially with a manhunt on the go. Maybe she wasn't so important to them, after all?

Swallowing the knock to her ego, she let herself into the office. The lights came on.

A dozen armed guards in full tactical get-up pointed their weapons at her. Carlos sat back with his immaculate leather shoes resting on his desk. Burgess stood beside the desk, alongside...

Kat.

'Nice of you to join us,' Carlos said, his broad smile betraying how delighted he was at the turn of events. 'I thought it would take you less time to come back to us. Clearly I overestimated your skills.' He turned to Burgess. 'Perhaps we had little to worry about.'

'You bitch,' Lois hissed at Burgess. 'You killed my wife.'

'I think you'll find there's no evidence to support your assertion, officer,' Burgess replied, a smile on her face.

Lois turned back to Carlos. 'I watched her'—she motioned to Burgess, who had the gall to look affronted—'murder my wife, and as soon as I get the chance, I'm going to rip out her throat and stamp on her lungs.'

'Officer!' Burgess said, half laughing. 'Hardly language becoming of an agent of Interpol.'

'You've murdered three of our agents, one of your own staff, and let's not forget my wife. I'll say whatever I goddamn please,' Lois spat back. She turned to Kat. 'And as for you...'

'For the record,' Carlos said, 'and for any government agency listening, we deny involvement in any of the crimes of which Agent Pertin accuses us of. In fact, we are of the belief she is the one guilty of trying to...'

'I watched it happen.' Lois scrambled, trying to work out Carlos's play.

Kat stood alongside Burgess, saying nothing.

'You don't seriously believe we go around murdering people, do you? This is business, not some kind of criminal enterprise. Besides, how can we have killed your wife, when she's right here?'

A door on the far side of the room opened. A soldier marched Marisa through. Her face was badly bruised, and her dark hair was dank, unwashed. But she was alive. Her eyes looked around wildly, trying to take in her surroundings, until they landed on Lois.

'Marisa!' Lois said, making to cross the room to her. Instead, every gun in the place raised as one, pointing either at Lois or at Marisa. Lois froze, turning to Kat. Her gun pointed straight at Lois's head.

Relief flooded over her, crashing like a wave. Marisa was alive. Nothing else mattered for a split second—until she remembered everything that did. Her girls. Justice.

Revenge.

'Don't be so surprised,' Carlos said, the smile returning to his face. 'We figured there was only one way to get you here, but we're not complete savages.'

Lois ignored him, looking instead at her wife. 'Are you okay?'

Marisa nodded; eyes fixed on Lois.

'The girls?'

Marisa nodded again.

Lois turned back to Carlos. 'You've got me here. So, what?'

'We want to know exactly what Interpol thinks it knows.'

'That it?'

He shrugged.

Lois chanced it. This whole thing had gone southward enough to warrant a Hail Mary. 'Fine. We know about the Minos. Christopher Sun can expect a visit any day.'

Carlos sneered. 'I see. What exactly is it you think you know about the Minos mission? I'd hate to think you're fishing for information.'

'You admit there is something about the Minos mission severe enough to have Christopher Sun worried?'

Carlos laughed. 'Nice try. I applaud you. Unfortunately, your friend here...'—he motioned to Kat—'told us you have nothing substantial. We needed to be sure. We may have fooled you with a vid, but if I were to stand up....' He stood, opening a drawer in his ornate desk, reaching inside to pull out a gun. '...and put this to your darling wife's temple, would you still answer the same?'

'You played me?' Lois asked Kat.

'I know which side my bread is buttered.' She didn't even have the grace to look ashamed.

'The Detective here reached out to us earlier today. She discovered you conspiring against the great city of Atlanta and played along so she could deliver you to us. She arrived on the scene with a squadron of Atlanta PD's finest, and they will testify to anything which goes on in this room, however it shakes out.'

'I'm sorry, for what it's worth,' Kat said. She pulled out the data stick recording proceedings and dropped it, crushing it beneath her boot.

Lois spat on the floor.

'There are two options here,' Burgess said. 'One, you tell us everything you know, and agree your report into Sunset is a dead end. We will bind you to never speak of anything you've heard inside this building, or outside, relating to Sunset. In return, we will let you, and your family, leave the city. But know this—our reach is beyond anything you can dream of. You break the agreement; we will break ours. You have a beautiful family, Lois.'

'What's the other option?' Lois asked.

'You don't want to find out, do you?' Carlos said.

'No,' Burgess said. 'She needs to know what the stakes are here. First, I will blow your wife's brains over the floor, and give you a second time to grieve her before I do the same to yours. After your funerals, I will take those two darling children of yours to one of our plantations in Eastern Europe, where they will become slaves. They will work there every day until they die. Don't worry, it'll be quicker than you'd think. Life expectancy is around forty years.'

A shudder crawled along Lois's spine.

'You're willing to do that with this many witnesses?' Lois asked, motioning to the Atlanta PD officers who still had their guns firmly trained on her.

'These fine officers are about to find themselves employees of Sunset Secure,' Burgess said. 'I'm confident they'll see which way the wind blows. This is our town. You think you can send your little spies here to snoop around, think you can con your way inside our family, and there won't be consequences?'

Lois stood for a moment, considering. She sighed. 'Kat?' she asked.

'Yeah, I think we have it.' Kat wheeled round, smashing Burgess on the head with the butt of her pistol.

Burgess fell to the ground in a slump. Across the other side of the desk, Marisa screamed into her gag.

Carlos staggered backward. 'Guards, seize her!' he shouted, but the guards stayed still.

Kat laughed. 'Carlos, these aren't your guards. These are officers of the Atlanta PD. You may think those two groups are interchangeable, but I can assure you they're not. At least, not all of them.'

Lois rushed to Marisa, taking the binds off her wrists and mouth. She pulled her into an embrace, but her wife pulled away, horrified.

'What the hell have you got us into?'

'Where are the girls?'

'Somewhere else in the building, I think. That woman... I think she knew where.'

'Okay, we'll worry about them in a minute.'

'I'm sure Carlos here knows,' Kat said, moving round to him, back in his chair, his eyes frantically searching for an exit.

He lunged for his intercom, but Kat caught his hand, twisting it back until it shattered in a noisy crack of bones.

'We wouldn't want to be interrupted, would we?' she said. 'Not before we've found out what was worth killing three Interpol agents for.'

Chapter Ten

G unfire crackled across the dormitory under the sound of Mercy's screams, shattering the windows. The children's screams joined with Mercy's, diving for the floor. Judd crawled behind a bed, peering underneath to see what was going on. Across the room, shielded from the guns by a flimsy wire bed frame, the children huddled into a ball of hospital gowns and tiny limbs, weeping in a clump of terror. The soldiers opened fire as a warning shot, and sunk to their knees to establish a line against the terrified children. Between them, Lan and the two other teeps stood firm.

Lan raised her hands and pointed them toward the soldiers. They slid across the floor, back toward the door.

Mercy's screams did not diminish. She stood on the bed; hands balled up into fists. Her wail was a siren, rebounding off the walls.

A soldier made to ready a weapon against her, not the machine gun of his compatriots, but what looked like a cannon. A rubber bullet gun.

'No!' Judd shouted.

Lan turned her attention to the soldier, lifting her hand up. The soldier fired, shooting high and wide over the small girl.

Immediately, Mercy stopped screaming, her attention going to her attacker. She didn't raise her hands as Judd had seen other teeps do. Her power seemed all in her eyes.

The soldier's hands, shaking, turned the gun round, loading another rubber round into the chamber as he went. Panic crossed his face. He grimaced and screamed as he tried to stop.

The barrel moved in front of his face.

'Mercy, stop,' Lan shouted, but the girl ignored him.

The soldier fired, the rubber round connecting with his face in a sickening crunch of bones and brains, the latter splattering over the wall behind him. His body slumped backward, dead.

The soldier next to him scrambled away, covered in gore, dropping his weapon. The other soldiers held firm, a line of black, their guns raised in unison.

Mercy turned her attention to them. Weapons vibrated in their hands. One soldier dropped his gun, scrambling back on all fours. She made to get out of the room, but Mercy slammed the doors shut.

'Fire at will,' a soldier shouted, voice trembling with panic. But no bullets came.

Barrels turned in shaking hands. One soldier sobbed, begging. Others stared forward, trying to reclaim their brains, trying to stop it.

'Mercy, please, don't do this,' Judd said. 'You don't have to.'

'Judd,' Lan said, struggling with her own gift against Mercy's, trying to pull the weapons away to no avail. 'Do it.'

Judd took a breath, the light growing within him. It no longer scared him, no longer took him over, so he let it swell.

'Quickly,' Lan shouted. Judd looked over the glow emanating from his chest. The gun barrels were almost level with the soldier's faces, sweat pouring off them, grimaces worn on each one as they fought the little girl in their heads.

Judd took a deep breath and directed the wave of light to Mercy. She crumpled, falling sideways off the bed like a rag doll. The huddled mass of children cowering across the room broke apart, wailing, rushing over to the fallen child.

Free of the fog Mercy had them under, the soldier's barrels turned back to the children.

'No,' Judd cried. 'Get the fuck out of here.'

Lan set her feet into a firm stance and held both hands out together. The soldiers skidded back toward the wall. She'd bought them a second, maybe two.

The doors slammed open. Judd's heart sank for a moment as more uniforms flooded through until he realised they belonged to the students. Teeps.

His people.

The soldiers, already off guard, stumbled back, waving their guns about to get the students to back down. One tall student took a soldier down with a hard right hook that lifted the soldier off his feet even with the riot gear, while another stepped forward, a TK, and lifted three soldiers into the air with a wave of his hands, dropping them on their heads with a crack. It was over in a few moments, and seven bodies lay on the ground. Judd hoped they weren't dead.

'What happened?' one student, the one with the powerful right hook, asked Bertrand.

'Soldiers came in here, looking for the kids. Went straight for Mercy.'

'What the fuck is he doing here?' another newcomer, a tall woman with red hair, asked, giving Judd a look that told him everything he needed to know.

'He shut Mercy down,' Lan said, crossing to where Mercy had fallen. The other children let her through, and Lan touched her face, closing her eyes as she did so. 'She's fine,' she said, opening her eyes. 'She blacked out.'

'That we know of,' Bertrand said. 'We don't know what he did.'

Strong-right-hook walked over to Judd, staring him down. Not a hard job, given the extra half a foot he had on Judd. 'This piece of shit do it again?'

'He had no choice,' Lan said, lifting Mercy's frail body back onto the bed, laying her down. 'Back off, okay?'

'Why?' the redhead asked.

'She made them put their own gun barrels in their mouths. She was going to kill them. In front of these kids.'

'He should have let her,' Bertrand said, his eyes fixed on Judd.

Judd realised half a beat too late what was about to happen.

Strong-right-hook lunged forward. Judd's jaw shattered as his fist connected, and he flew backward to rendezvous with the floor.

His head hit hard, but he had no time for the spinning world of blinding pain which threatened to engulf him. He held his arms up to ward off the attackers descending upon him, but they ignored his flailing hands and howls of pain.

The redhead was up next, kicking out with a boot which caught his already broken lower ribs. She kept kicking until Bertrand stepped forward. He stamped on Judd's knee, sending a blast of pain so bad it almost knocked him out.

Judd tried to say something, anything, to make them stop, but nothing came out but a splutter of blood and teeth. He tried the defence of limply holding his hand out to get them to stop a second time. It met a stomped boot, breaking his hand, and another to the face, sending him sliding backward into one of the metal bed frames.

At least he was out of their immediate reach.

'Stop!' The voice of Walker called out. The room fell silent.

Judd tried to pick himself up, but fell down before he could start.

'What the hell is going on here?' Walker hissed.

Judd tried to focus. His three assailants stood a few feet away, barely restraining their hatred toward him behind scowls. Behind them, other students hung back. The children had reformed their terror ball, while Lan tended to Mercy. She hadn't tried to intervene in the stomping he'd received.

In the doorway, a horrified Walker sat in his chair, Mrs Smith beside him. Judd's heart soared. They'd save him.

He tried to speak but only brought up blood, which dribbled down his chin.

'That fuck took Mercy out,' Bertrand replied, pointing at Judd. Unnecessary, Judd thought. They knew who he was talking about.

'Is she okay?' Walker asked Lan.

She nodded. 'I think so.'

'We have to go,' Mrs Smith said. 'The last glide is waiting. There are soldiers all over the campus, looking for her.'

'Yes,' Walker said. He turned to the other teeps. 'Gather the children. Bertrand, can you carry Mercy?'

'Sure,' Bertrand said, shooting Judd a last look before picking the frail child up.

What about him? Why was nobody concerned about him? He tried to ask, but all that came out was a low, toothless moan.

The teeps gathered up the children and left the dormitory. Nobody made a move to help Judd. Mrs Smith didn't give him so much as a backward glance.

He tried again to get to his elbows but fell back down, the pain so unbearable he could barely keep a grasp on consciousness. His eyelids were so heavy they forced themselves closed, despite his frantic effort to keep them open. He was about to die.

Before he slid under, Walker moved over toward him.

'I'm sorry,' Walker said. 'I just don't know how to keep you in our world, kid.'

He turned away as Judd slid into darkness.

Chapter Eleven

'Lois,' Marisa hissed, 'let's get out of here, okay?'

'Not yet,' Lois said. 'This motherfucker has our girls, and I want to know why he feels a photo I don't even understand is important enough to kidnap them. And you. This... pig, he made me watch you die to get me to come in. I had to watch that, Marisa. He's going to pay.' She was struggling to control her voice, she knew, but she didn't care.

'Ladies, please,' Carlos pleaded, his eyes darting around the room for any exit he might take. 'I'm a father, too.'

'No, you're not,' Lois replied. 'Or didn't you think I did my research on every single one of you? Tell me what the photo means, and why it was worth going to all this trouble, or I'll have Kat here shoot you in the face. Right between the eyes. Oh,' she said, pulling out her pad and tapping a button. 'Make sure you speak loud and clear for the record.'

'You women are insane,' he stammered, indignant. 'I don't know what you're talking about.'

'Oh yeah?' Lois said. 'Marisa can testify you kidnapped her and her daughters—my daughters—held her against her will, and took those girls away. I have several police officers here who will swear, under oath, that you threatened to kill two innocent children. I think even someone as powerful as yourself might find it hard to get a DA to plea that away.'

Carlos paused, eyes darting from the armed guards, to Lois, to Kat. 'If I tell you where your daughters are, will you let me go?'

'Commander,' a soldier said, his finger to his ear. 'Chief is sending reinforcements.'

Kat frowned. 'I don't think they'll be here to help us take this prick into custody. We need to move. He's not going to tell us anything.'

'Sure he is,' Lois said, taking the pistol from Kat, and holding it to Carlos's temple. 'You're going to tell us what that picture was.'

'A family barbecue, that's all,' Carlos stammered in response.

'Bullshit,' Lois said. She took the pistol and slammed the butt down on Carlos's hand, hard. He screamed, a howl of anguished pain which lasted far longer than Lois wanted it to. She leaned in. 'What was that meeting about? Why were the Minos crew meeting with Christopher Sun?'

The office door opened, and the most powerful man in the world walked through.

Christopher Sun, his grey suit matching both the grey of his hair and the silver of the pistol he held to Rosa's temple. Lois's daughter stood, whimpering, while her other daughter, Stacey, stood frozen in fear. Both looked dirty, tired, and like they'd been crying for days.

Sun smiled, a wide smile full of too many teeth. 'If I told you it was because I wanted to meet with the brave astronauts before they went up, you wouldn't believe me?' he called out, voice booming with grandeur. He walked in with an effortless swagger, even as he ushered in the two children at gunpoint.

'Mama,' Rosa said weakly at his side.

'Now,' Sun said. 'Let's see if we can negotiate a way out of this.' There was his wide smile again. Lois might have found it disarming if he didn't have a gun to her daughter's head.

Lois looked to Marisa, who stood horrified, tears streaming down her face. Marisa moved toward the girls, but Sun raised the pistol.

'That's far enough.' When Marisa stopped, the pistol went back to Rosa's head. Lois's stomach turned.

'Okay,' she said, and dropped the pistol on the floor.

The police officers, their attention caught between Carlos and Sun, lowered their barrels.

'Good,' Sun said. He moved the pistol away from Rosa's head. 'Let's see if we can talk like sensible adults here.'

The girls ran toward Marisa, who scooped them both up in her arms and turned her back on the rest of the room. On Lois.

'I'm listening,' Lois said.

'Well, simply, you can leave.'

'Just like that?'

'You'll have to leave the chip, and any listening devices, but essentially, yes. You have my deepest sympathies for your treatment. There will be an internal investigation into the events which transpired here, but you'll appreciate that given the sensitivity of the timing, Sunset Industries will not be subjecting itself to external scrutiny at this time.' He put his pistol away, straightened his suit jacket, and flashed them a curt smile.

Lois shook her head. The fucking audacity.

'You killed four people,' Kat said, incredulous. 'Do you think we'll let them slide?'

'Ah, well, I think you'll find those killings were an over-zealous security officer. You seem to have dealt with her already.' He motioned to Burgess's lifeless body, somewhat forgotten on the floor.

'No,' Lois said. Slowly, pieces came together, in a way they never had before. 'No, Burgess didn't kill them. She threatened me with a gun, not a knife. Those bodies had cuts from ear to ear. It's a brutal crime. But Burgess's instincts went straight to a gun. You hired out the killings. Or you contracted them to someone within Sunset Secure.'

Sun's lips curled into a sneering smile. 'Prove it.'

Lois thought about moving, about leaving the room, but something inside her couldn't get her to move. Instinct, perhaps. She smiled at him. 'Well, it's very kind of you to let us all leave. We'll be off in just a moment. But first, I'm still trying to work out why you'd go to this much trouble over a simple picture.'

Sun stared at her; the smile gone from his face.

'Young lady,' Sun started, but didn't seem to have anything to follow up on, so Lois ploughed on.

'It's not so much the photo. I buy you inviting the crew over. But why was this photo buried in a sub-folder of the Sunset archives dedicated to research into the Mar? A folder which pre-dated the public declaration of the Mar by some time, but that's by-the-by.'

Sun sneered, his wide mouth full of teeth appearing briefly beneath thin lips. He tilted his head at Lois, as though sizing her up, or perhaps deciding how she might taste. The smile faded, and he stuck out his chin. 'We discovered the Mar, and tried to come up with a solution before it went public,' Sun said in a low voice, not cowed but choosing his words carefully. It was a contrast to the booming power of his usual public voice. It told Lois she was on the right course.

'Is that so?' she asked. 'Because it would beg the question—how did you discover the Mar, exactly?'

'Where are you going with this, Detective?' Sun asked, feigning incredulity.

'There's some reason you don't want that picture spread around, that's for damn sure,' Marisa said. Their girls hung onto the hem of her dress, staring out with wide, wild eyes. Lois knew she should get them out of here, but she had to know. If she left this room without the truth, it was for nothing.

'Holy shit,' Lois said, as a realisation hit like a thunderbolt. Sun's face fell. 'Ermine,' she continued. 'The Second Officer. Seeing you and him together—he's yours, isn't he? You're the second Christopher Sun, right? Your father started the company, mad bastard that he was, but you inherited it. Those rumours about your father, his theories of depopulation. You took over and washed it away. But whatever you've done, Ermine is the one cleaning up after you, isn't he? He looks so much like you it's crazy. What's the matter, did he piss you off so much he didn't get the family name?'

Sun laughed, shaking his head. 'Oh, Detective, how little you know. How little any of you know.' He motioned to the wide, dark window behind Carlos's desk. 'You see the world out there? It's dying. Humanity killed it. The sole hope any of has is to strip things back, start over, do things better. This insignificant planet of ours cannot sustain the ever-growing population we keep foisting on it. Even through everything that's happened—floods, famines, wars—the needle has barely moved on keeping the global population under control. So I acted. Like I always have. It might have gotten away from me, but at least I tried. And we will fix it. We will make it better.'

'Sir,' Carlos said, from his chair, nursing his broken hand. 'I must insist on stopping you.'

Sun gave his subordinate a disingenuous smile, as though he'd finished a nice after-party tale, and clapped his hands together. 'If you don't mind, Carlos and I have some things to be getting on with and I don't want to have to deal with a load of corpses in my own headquarters. You're free to go. I'd advise you to get as much of a head start as you can. Carlos, shall we?'

Carlos leapt out of his chair, still holding his hand, which looked pretty fucked up, Lois noted with not a little satisfaction.

Sun and Carlos left the office, leaving the rest of them in silence. Kat's officers lowered their weapons completely. 'What do we do, Detective?' one of them asked.

'We need to get out of here,' Kat said.

'He's not going to let us go,' Lois said. 'We'll be dead before we hit the parking lot. He didn't even take the pad.'

'Lois,' Marisa said. 'Can we please get our girls out of here?'

'Sure,' Lois said. 'Sorry.' She reached forward to put her fingers through Stacey's hair, but she pulled away, clinging to Marisa.

'Come on,' Kat said.

Chapter Twelve

The darkness was absolute, the tube so narrow Wyn couldn't move—an endless ride in a plastic coffin. She struggled to breathe, struggled to keep hold of her sense of self. Tried to count to ten out loud, as much to keep herself from screaming as anything else. Tears ran down her cheeks, into her mouth. Her nose ran like a broken faucet as she tried to keep a grip. She focused on the numbers.

'One.'

'Two.'

'Three.'

The sobbing returned. When would this end? Was she gaining speed? Putting her hand out to steady herself, it made no impact, her knuckles dragging along the imperfections in the plastic.

She began to black out, aware enough to think it might not be the worst idea in the world. Thoughts beyond that failed to form in her mind. She forced her eyes closed again and waited for the impact.

Shooting out into open air, she slammed into something head first, sending pricks of light darting behind her closed eyes. She opened them, woozily trying to take in her surroundings. A large room pooled with water and filled with harsh white light. The rest of the crew around her in various states of disarray.

Her headset filled with the noise of their radios as the link between them came back. Someone screamed.

Zoe.

Barnes attended to her, fashioning a splint. There were droplets of blood in the water.

Stef powered through the knee high water toward Wyn as she sank to the floor. Wyn's hands still shook, her breath coming in shallow sobs.

'Jesus, Wyn, are you okay?' she said.

'I'm fine,' Wyn replied, weakly.

'You were screaming.'

'I'm fine,' Wyn said, trying to compose herself. 'It's just... I'm not great with close spaces. Or water.'

'Oh,' Stef said, helping Wyn to her feet. 'This is the perfect mission for you, eh?'

'Don't I know it?' Wyn muttered.

Behind them, a surge of water heralded the Captain's arrival. He skidded across the floor gracefully, before getting to his feet as though he'd stepped out of a plush limousine.

'Everyone made it?' he said, looking around. 'What's our status?'

'Zoe's hurt,' Barnes said. 'I need to get her to med bay.'

'I'll be fine,' Zoe hissed, pulling herself up onto her good leg with a wince of pain.

'Li, how are we getting on?'

It was the first time Wyn noticed Li wasn't there.

'Glad you're here,' Li said, over comms. 'I think you'd better come and see this.'

The habitat, known as Haven, was extraordinary. Wyn had heard Stef and Li talk about it, had seen the diagrams, but nothing could prepare her for the world crafted for them. The crew arrived through the pipe into a section designed to pump the water under the ice into a loop, giving them the pressure they needed to transport down here. It would take them back to the surface too. But this chamber was only the beginning.

There were six individual pods, each bigger than their stations on the Minos. Each pod connected to the seventh—the main deck—which operated as a central hub. The other pods radiated from the centre like spokes on a wheel—two bunks, a science pod for Zoe, a cargo pod, a mess, and a med bay.

'How the hell did you manage to get this down here?' Wyn asked. She'd imagined tiny, cramped spaces. 'I mean, how the hell did this fit in the Andy?'

'Spatial dynamic structures,' Stef replied, as they walked through to the central hub. 'A flat pack living space. The entire structure folds down into a solid mass one thousandth the size. Technically, we could reprogram the polymers into any configuration we want.'

'A theory probably best not tested while we're inside it,' Hamza said.

Li stood at the far side of the room, his hands on a panel, a wry smirk on his face. His helmet was off. 'Took you guys long enough,' he said. 'I was wondering if I'd have to do the entire mission myself.'

'You could have banged on the pipe to let us know you were alright,' Hamza said, taking his own helmet off and giving Li a hug.

The rest of the crew removed their helmets, Barnes sniffing the air suspiciously as he did so.

'Everything deployed properly?' Captain Davis asked.

'Absolutely fine.'

'I need to get Zoe to med bay,' Barnes said.

'Well, if she's okay to wait a minute, I think there's something she'd like to see,' Li said, his smirk intensifying.

'What have you got, Li?' Ermine said, somewhat impatiently.

'Look at your feet,' Li said.

The floor beneath them was black, but closer inspection revealed the swirl of water pressing against it, dark and unforgiving. If it impressed Li, it scared the living crap out of Wyn. She nearly jumped up onto a chair, but composed herself.

'I give you,' Li said with a flourish, 'the underwater ocean of Europa.'

He flicked a button on the panel. Lights flared up below their feet, illuminating the ocean outside.

Wyn stepped back, wanting even more to jump on a chair. Beside her, Barnes gasped.

Below their feet, in water so clear it looked like air, lay a world of wonder.

'Holy shit,' Zoe said, almost giggling as she stepped forward on her damaged leg to view the multitude of life-forms surrounding them.

Fish, eels, what looked like mammals, plankton, coral—they'd stumbled into a diverse ecosystem beyond even their home's oceans. Every being in front of them looked like some distant relation of something back on Earth, and yet... everything was white. Nothing seemed to have any pigment.

A hundred metres away from Haven was the face of a mountain, its hard rock jutting into the hard crust of ice above them, the source of the fissure they'd exploited. Life buzzed around the mountainside, with white coral peppering the rocks, and what looked vaguely like fish feeding off it. Then, in the waters around them—the creatures.

Below the ice they looked an almost entirely different animal, like the ghost of a manatee. With the claws and teeth no longer visible, in the water they had movement quite unlike their violent motions out on the ice.

They swam in packs, like a shoal, oblivious, like the rest of the life down there, to the human beings invading their world.

'My God,' Zoe said. 'It's unlike anything we could have imagined.'

'Why aren't they reacting to the lights?' Wyn asked.

'They have no use for sight,' Zoe replied. 'There's no light down here, so the entire ecosystem has developed without it. It's why there's no pigment, too. Fauna, flora, it's surviving on something other than sunlight down here.'

'You'd best get to work, doc,' Ermine said. 'Let's get you patched up first, eh?'

Barnes and Ermine led Zoe away. Li extinguished the lights. Wyn breathed a sigh of relief. None of it enchanted her. It was terrifying, like living on a glass-bottomed boat, except everything under the glass was horrifically alien.

Part of her unease was the gravity. After three years of zero gravity on the Minos, the sudden reappearance of it this close to the moon's core felt like walking around with a backpack full of bricks. Her bones ached, and her muscles felt ill-equipped to deal with the pressure resting on them.

The room emptied. Everyone else had work to be getting on with. Her, not so much. There was nothing left to do. Nothing except wrestling with the knowledge someone had tried to kill her. Someone willing to throw the entire mission under a bus.

This should be the proudest moment of her life. She was a pioneer. She'd flown farther than anyone in human history and discovered a holy grail at the end of the trip. But she didn't much feel like celebrating.

She walked over to a chair and sat, staring at the floor and the murk beneath. She guessed it was down to her to find out who'd tried to kill them.

It was possible the answer would spell the end of humanity itself.

Chapter Thirteen

Kat's cabal of loyal Atlanta PD officers led the way, forming a circle around Lois, Marisa, and the girls. Lois did not know where Kat dragged them up from—she'd kept that part of their plan secret. Whoever they were, they were loyal to Kat, or at least, weren't loyal to Sunset. They looked to Kat for orders, and she kept them in check with tiny nods and gestures.

They worked their way down the corridor in silence, moving through the hallway, checking every door for danger. They reached the elevators unmet by security or other foes.

There wasn't room in the elevators for all of them, so the officers went first, leaving two behind to wait for the next elevator with Lois and the others.

They rode down in silence, each deep in their own thoughts. Lois tried to unpick Sun's words. If they could make it out of the building unmolested—and it was an almighty if—it was her duty to get the word out. Tell Interpol. Tell the world. She had the most powerful man in the world, on tape, admitting to... what, exactly?

Shit.

She fished out the pad and the chip, sliding the latter into the case of the former, and tucking both into her back pocket. There was plenty of time to unpick what Sun had said once they got the hell out of here.

The doors opened to the long wide lobby and its panoramic view of the city, now viewed through glass cracked and shattered by the earlier explosion. Despite the damaged glass, Lois could still see the long line of armed police, their weapons raised.

Kat's officers stood behind a wall, shielded from the view of their colleagues. Lois picked up Stacey, checked Marisa had Rosa and crossed the space, eyes never straying from the window. The police out there must have seen them, but made no move.

'Shit,' Kat asked, peering round the corner of the wall. 'Our own PD?'

'Looks like it,' an officer confirmed.

'Get them on the line.'

He nodded and held his finger to his ear. 'This is Tré, who's the OIC out there?'

They waited in silence, all eyes on the officer. Marisa stood behind Lois, their girls cowering behind her legs.

'I don't like this,' Marisa said.

'Yes, sir,' Barker said, and took his finger away. 'Chief's out there. Says to come out, unarmed.'

'How did he sound?' Kat asked.

'Pissed,' Barker said. 'Listen, Commander, I report to you, but if the Chief says come out, we come out. Besides, we're witnesses to what Sun said up there. That's a hell of a lot of us to silence.'

'That's what worries me,' Kat said. 'Okay. Let's move out.'

'You ladies stay behind us, okay?' Barker said. Lois nodded.

The officers moved forward in formation, picking their way across the lobby. Lois and the others tucked in behind them as instructed. As they moved forward Lois felt a tiny hand grab her own, and looked down to see Rosa looking up, her face a mask of fear.

'It's okay sweetie, we'll be out of here soon enough.'

If only she believed it herself. Where the hell were Sunset's security?

They reached the front of the lobby. The security gates were open—doors, too, leaving an unimpeded view of the line of police officers outside.

Movement caught her eye, off to her left.

Out of sight of the assembled police, flat on the floor. Two Sunset guards, their weapons pointed at the officers outside.

'No!' Lois shouted, but it was already too late.

The Sunset guards opened fire with a staccato burst, spraying bullets indiscriminately across the police line outside.

Kat's officers froze halfway across the lobby, caught desperately out in the open.

Sunset's bullets found their marks, taking down three separate officers outside, shattering another window.

'Return fire,' the call came out. Across from them, the police opened fire.

'No!' Lois shouted.

The girls screamed; their anguish audible over even the sounds of gunfire echoing across the wide lobby.

One officer, Lois thought it might be Tré, waved his arms in a signal to his brethren to hold fire. A bullet tore through his throat. He fell backwards, dead.

Lois, Marisa, and the girls fell to the ground, confused, terrified. They crawled, a daughter each under their arms, away from the gunfire. Kat followed, but got pinned down halfway to safety by gunfire. She hid behind an overturned chair, scant cover if anyone were to open fire.

Lois and Marisa found their way behind a wall. They sat, panting.

'What do we do?' Marisa asked. Between the two of them, their daughters curled into sobbing, wailing balls.

'I don't know,' Lois said. 'Kat?'

'Yeah?' Kat called back, unseen by both of them.

'Any ideas?'

'Not really.'

'Okay.'

Lois looked back to Marisa and her two girls. 'I'm sorry I dragged you into this.'

Lois reached out her hand, and Marisa took it in her own and gave it a squeeze. Rosa cuddled up into Lois, and for a moment Lois forgot where she was.

A volley of gunfire slammed into the wall a few feet over.

Kat burst into view, sliding across the floor and round the corner.

'Let's get the fuck out of here, shall we?' she said.

'It's definitely a plan. How?' Lois replied.

'I took out the two sniper fucks. We need to convince the cops to stop firing.'

'Can't you talk to them?'

'They're jamming my signal. Or someone is.'

'How can you know who to trust?' Marisa asked.

Kat shook her head. 'We can't. Is there no other way out?'

Lois wracked her brains. 'Nothing we can reach.'

'You in there,' a man's voice called out over a loudspeaker. 'Is there anyone still alive in there?'

'No,' Kat called out.

'Who is that?' the voice replied.

'Stone. Who's that?'

'Chief Douglas.'

'Hey, Chief.'

Silence.

'How about you give yourselves up?' the Chief replied.

'We tried to. Everyone started shooting,' Kat shouted back. 'You got suckered in by Sunset's security. They opened fire on you.'

'Uh huh?'

'Look,' Kat said. 'We're happy to come out and talk to you about it, as long as you agree not to shoot us.'

'We won't shoot if you don't.'

'We have kids in here, Chief. I need your word.'

'You have it.'

Kat looked at Lois and shrugged. 'I don't see another way out of here, okay?'

Lois nodded and turned to Marisa. 'Stay here, stay down, until we're safely out the door, okay?'

'Wait, no, I want to come with you.'

Lois placed her hand on Marisa's shoulder. 'You'll be with me in a few minutes, okay?' She took the pad out of her pocket, lowering her head and looking directly into Rosa's eyes. 'Sweetie, can you do something for me? Can you look after this?'

Rosa nodded, the motion sending tiny droplets of tears and snot falling onto her top. She took the pad, gripping it so tight her knuckles turned white.

Lois gathered her girls into a tight embrace. 'I love you, so much,' she said, struggling to keep her voice even. She looked up into Marisa's eyes. 'If anything happens, you run. Okay? I don't know how, but get out of here. I'll find you, if I can.'

Marisa nodded. Lois kissed her, both their lips wet and salty. She savoured the moment as long as she could.

Kat stood, tucking her pistol inside her waistband. 'Let's do this.'

They stood up and shook themselves off. Both raised their hands. 'We're coming out,' Kat said.

They advanced round the corner.

The glass front to the building was obliterated. Between them and the doors, the bodies of Kat's men lay bloodied and dead. Cops killed by cops. Beyond the empty windows, the line stood firm, their weapons pointed at the pair of them. Amid them stood a man, his uniform barely creased amongst the pitch black of his officers' Swat outfits.

'Chief,' Kat said.

'Detective. Told you you'd find yourself in bother.'

'Before we get into that, I need to tell you. I'm actually not working for your department. I work for Interpol. As does my colleague here. We're both investigating Sunset.'

'That right?'

'It is.' Lois confirmed. 'We've got evidence directly implicating Christopher Sun in crimes against humanity. We're going to need your help to…'

'Let me stop you there,' the Chief said, holding his hands up. 'We can get into it down at the station. This all there is of you?'

Lois nodded.

'If you've got evidence, hand it over.' He held his hand out. There was still a good five metres between them, but it was clear he wouldn't move closer.

'Chief,' Kat said. 'Please, don't do this.'

'This is too important, Kat.'

Kat looked at Lois with horror in her eyes.

The guns opened fire. A bullet to the cheek cut Kat down, sending her flying backward. Two more bullets found her before her body hit the floor.

A bullet slammed into Lois's shoulder, spinning her round. A second went into her side. It was like plunging into ice water. She hit the floor with a crash that might well have hurt, if the rest of her wasn't already screaming with pain.

She looked back at the wall hiding Marisa and the girls, and hoped they were already running. It was the last thought she would have before the dark claimed her.

Chapter Fourteen

The hiss of the ventilator became Judd's sole companion. He was awake, but the doctors had to do... something medical... with his jaw, or he wouldn't be able to breathe properly. This afternoon, apparently. In the meantime, he had to lie on his own in a hospital room. Where, he didn't know. Stewing. Anger washed over him, freshly unearthed in every moment, every hour, every day that passed. He wanted to rip the tubes out. To scream at the world. But he couldn't move.

The doctors placed a view screen in his eyeline and wedged the control under his right hand. He refused to turn it on. Distraction wasn't what he wanted. He didn't want entertaining; he wanted to feel every trace of hate. Every ounce of pain.

What happened to him after the teeps left him to die was hazy. A fog. He spent days trying to piece it together.

Flashing lights. Blurs of movement. Pain.

Voices. He remembered snippets and tried to stitch them together.

'...Glide came down somewhere about ten miles away...'

'...Troops en route...'

'...Anyone survived...'

A man's crisp voice, different from the others. 'I don't give a
shit about anyone but the girl.'

Soldiers. He remembered uniforms. The same as those who
attacked the compound. The teeps had gone; left him to die.
Judd keeping as still as possible, scared of what fresh pain the
soldiers would bring him. Hoping they'd think him dead and
leave him alone to get there on his own.

'Fucking hell,' the man's voice continued. An American like
him, from the south somewhere. 'Any of those bodies have puls-
es, Private?'

Were they talking about him?

'This one,' a woman replied.

'He awake?'

'No.'

'Wake him up.'

Silence for a moment, and a startled gurgle.

'Sergeant, how are you doing?'

'Um, I... what the hell happened?'

'Hoping you could tell us.'

'They ambushed us, sir.'

'The girl?'

'At first, but one of them stopped her. Others came in, and...
that's all I remember, sir.'

'Well done, Sergeant.' He paused for a second. 'You said a teep
stopped her?'

'Yes, sir.'

'How?'

'I don't know. She was about to make me eat a bullet, sir. But
one of them shut her right off... like, completely.'

'Interesting. You be able to ID them?'

'No need, sir. That's him.'

Footsteps crossed over toward him.

'Jesus,' he said. 'They didn't take kindly to him intervening on your behalf, Sergeant. Private, get a medic up here, would you?'

'Yes, sir.'

The figure leaned in. Judd tried to say something, but as he opened his mouth, a blast of fresh pain enveloped his head. He closed his eyes to block it out, to no avail.

'It's okay, son,' the voice said. 'We're going to get you seen to, don't you worry. I reckon you and I will have plenty to talk about.'

Judd tried to take it in, but everything was variations of pain. The world swam again, and the shutters came back down.

That was everything he remembered. A tapestry of memories that took weeks to recreate. Soldiers saved him. In a way. Lying motionless in this bed for endless days didn't feel like salvation. He couldn't move. Pain was everything now.

Well, almost everything.

He closed his eyes to find the kernel of his power. This was always the hardest part, locating it. Once he got a whiff, a tiny spark, he could nurture it, grow it. After weeks of practice, it was the only thing he could control. He grew the light, shaped it into a ball, moved it around in front of him, expanded it from a ball of bright white light to a sphere of gossamer-thin mist, then bring it back down, shrink it back down to a tiny light, and stow it away. He'd rest, find the spark, and start again.

It wasn't just practising his talent, or sharpening the knife he'd use to stick in the heart of every teep in the world. The glow seemed to help him heal. Speed it along, at least. In the light, the pain covering every inch of him dissipated. If he had the strength, he would cloak himself in it, leave the pain behind.

He put the light away, and the pain came back. As did the image of the bastards who put him there. Walker, turning his back on him. Mrs. Smith, not even giving him a second glance. Lan, who told him to take out Mercy and let him take the blame for it.

Mercy. She was the only one he didn't blame. Here in this bed he had time to unpack the burst of images he'd received when he touched her skin. They were memories. Hers. Not just memories, these were experiences, full flesh and blood. An ocean of sadness, swimming in the head of a girl far too young to have seen any of it.

Every time a memory surfaced—of injections into her skull while wide awake, or of machines which thrummed and banged, or of nurses who held her down, holding their batons inches from her face to get her to comply—he could feel her rage. It fed into his own. Her rage was not for the teeps, but for the soldiers, the humans who made her.

Judd wondered where he fit. Neither one nor the other. Separate. Divorced from his humanity. Adrift from his own kind. He was something else.

Something new.

The door swung open. A man in a black uniform walked in; a soldier, replete with sidearm and armour plating.

Judd recognised him. He'd been in a few times to see Judd. He never spoke, and when Judd tried to search the man's mind, he found it closed. It wasn't surprising; the best luck he'd had so far searching minds was the doctor treating him. He latched onto her revulsion at his appearance. That was a fun time.

The soldier pulled up a chair next to Judd, scrutinising him with fierce eyes. Judd tried to ignore him. He could still run his exercises, if someone was there. They'd only notice if they were a teep, and, well, that was a reaction he looked forward to seeing.

'You're going under the knife this afternoon, I understand,' the man said. If it was a question, he was wasting his time. Speech was beyond Judd now. Hell, he could barely lift a finger.

Hey, that was a point. He could lift a finger. He moved his index finger off the clicker for the view screen and tapped the metal frame of his bed with the end of his fingernail. It gave off a tiny sound, but the soldier smiled.

'Good. We've flown in some of the best surgeons in the world to help get you well, Judd.'

Judd had nothing to offer in response, so his finger lay still.

'Don't worry about medical bills. The company will take care of it. You've caused quite a stir around here. You're special.'

He leaned forward. Judd adjusted his head the tiny amount he could to get a better view of the soldier, but it pressed the pipe going down his throat against his windpipe, making him choke. The soldier stood up, adjusting Judd's head so he could breathe again. He sat back down.

'I know, it's a bitch. Wanting to speak, not being able to. Could be you're telling me to go fuck myself. Somehow, I doubt it. I don't think your fellow teeps exalted you, so...'

He leaned back again.

'If it were me, I'd be pissed. Shattered jaw, tongue half ripped off, hairline fracture of the skull, nasty internal haemorrhaging, seven broken ribs, a punctured lung, and a shattered kneecap. That's a hell of a beating. You're damn lucky to be alive. Or, you will be, once we get you off this machine.'

He stood and walked to the machine, caressing the top of it like an old friend.

Judd's eyes followed the man until he passed out of view. He wished the fucker would find a point and leave him alone.

'I'd like to know how you feel about the people who put you in here. Your fellow teeps. Except we don't know if they are your fellow teeps. I suspect you're not one of them. Your gift is no gift for them. It's a gift to the world.'

Here it was, then. The big pitch. Judd wasn't stupid enough to think this man was here for Judd's own wellbeing. He wanted something. Everyone wanted something from him. Probably these were the same people who tortured Mercy.

'You can do something we've only ever been able to do with a bullet. People and teeps, they can't exist, side by side. Society is built on a foundation of trust, and secrecy. We get to live our lives, nobody peering into our heads.'

He sat down. Judd kept staring at the ceiling. He already knew this. If this guy would come back in a few days, when he didn't have this damn tube in his throat, he could tell him.

'Like you,' the soldier continued. 'You took yourself off to the moon for privacy. Never interfered with anyone. No record of teep activity. Kept yourself to yourself. We should all be free to do the same. Don't you agree?'

Perhaps a confirmation would get rid of this guy, so he could go back to practicing with the light. He tapped on the frame. The soldier nodded to himself.

'Good.' He paused, a smile dancing around the edge of his mouth. 'I have a surprise for you.'

He tapped on the glass window behind him. A few moments later, the door opened.

Another soldier entered, a woman leading a prisoner, judging by the bright orange jumpsuit and the hood over their head.

The new soldier led the prisoner to a chair, unceremoniously dumped them into it and pulled the hood off.

Lan.

Wild-eyed. Half deranged.

Judd's heart quickened, but he wasn't sure what the feeling swelling in his chest was. Was it recognition of a familiar face, the childish crush he had on the woman? Or was it hatred?

Lan looked around wildly, eyes taking a moment to adjust to the light. The right side of her face was heavily grazed, her hair matted. She had thick silver tape across her mouth, a smear of red at the top where her nose had bled.

'You remember this one, then?' the first soldier said. 'I can tell. After they left you there to die, they took off in a glide. Took the kids. But there was a problem. The glide went down a few miles into the moors. By the time we got there, they were gone. Fled across the hills. But not this one. This one we found unconscious. Abandoned, just like you. We got a fright when she woke up and we realised what she could do. Nearly flung an entire squadron off the glide. The only thing which works is the hood. She needs to see what she's moving.'

The soldier stood, looming over Judd so their eyes couldn't help but meet.

'In a minute, she's going to remember what she can do, even with her restraints. She's probably worked out what you working for us would mean for her people. She could whip that tube out of your throat, let you drown in your own collapsed jaw. If I were you, I'd make damn sure she doesn't get the chance.'

Lan looked at Judd with total horror. She recognised him, even in his state.

She let out a low moan, trying to speak, but the tape over her mouth prevented it. No doubt she was screaming at him in her head, but he couldn't hear her. Wouldn't.

The sight of her turned his stomach. His heart pounded. He felt the shower of fists and kicks raining down on him once more. What had she done to help him? Nothing. She could have stopped them.

He remembered her staring as the boot came down, fracturing his skull.

'...wanted to see for ourselves whether you had the capabilities we think you...'

Judd blocked the soldier out. He didn't care what some soldier wanted—he was too angry. Finding the spark of light quicker than before, he let bloom like wildfire.

He took pleasure in the fear clear in Lan's eyes as she saw the light too. She looked around, trying to find anything she could throw, settling on an empty chair.

It vibrated, lifting from the ground. Too late. The light inside him turned to a fire, an incandescent heat pulsing through his veins. For a moment he wasn't strapped to a gurney, a pipe down his throat. He rose, majestic, fuelled by pure vengeance and rage.

The light grew so hot he thought it might consume him, but he would not let it go. He cultivated it. It burned, churning, swirling away.

Somewhere, Lan tried to throw the chair at him, but as it hit the growing light it fell to the floor by his bed.

He locked eyes with her, saw the pleading within them.

No.

He let the light go, directing it out with all the force he could muster; a torrent of pure energy flowing from him like a beacon, covering Lan with his pure and indignant fury.

On and on it crashed—pure, malevolent rage, every strand filling Judd with satisfaction as it rolled over Lan.

Screams filled the room, barely audible over the blood pounding in his ears and the rushing outpouring of hate.

It ebbed and was gone.

Judd was still on the bed. The tube was still in his throat. Everything still hurt.

What remained of Lan sat in the chair, blood running from her eyes, nose, and ears. He didn't know if she was dead, or if he'd snapped her mind, but she was gone. Anything still alive in there was nothing more than a husk. A shell.

He waited for the guilt. Where was the sense of regret?

Judd moved his finger over the pointer and used it to call up a text screen on the viewer. Slowly he moved his finger, painstakingly typing out three words.

The soldier—his chair fallen to the floor, his body pressed against the wall—stared at the broken bait he'd brought Judd, a look of terror on his smug face.

Judd finished. He stared forward at the screen at what he'd written.

The soldier tore his eyes away from Lan and looked up at the screen, and the three words displayed on it.

Bring me more.

Keep Reading

This is the end of Season One of The Sunset Chronicles
Season Two begins with...
A Dawn To Fear

Leave a review

I really hope you've enjoyed reading Season One of The Sunset Chronicles.

If you did, the nicest thing you could do for me right now is to leave a review, on all or any of the books. Reviews are absolutely crucial to discoverability, and social proof. If you could take a second to rate and review this at the store of your choice, I'd hugely appreciate it.

Thanks,
Paul

JOIN THE HOLLOW STONE

Join my reader's group
and be the first on the planet
to hear about new releases,
and get exclusive content
you won't find anywhere else.

Author's Note

As a kid who went to boarding school, the holidays were difficult for me. Not because of having to be away from school – far from it, because that place was a dumpster fire – but because I didn't have friends where I lived. My nearest friends were inevitably a good half an hour away by train, or they lived in Scotland, or somewhere in the home counties. Even when I lived in London the other kids who in the city never lived in the same part of the sprawling metropolis as me, so while we could maybe meet up occasionally and bum around the Trocadero Centre playing on the arcades, most days over the long summer break were spent at home. Alone. But I didn't have it as bad as some.

For instance, there was a kid I had an on/off friendship with whose parents lived in Germany. He was a forces kid, and so while I had it bad enough in London, he had it immeasurably worse. He had to hop on a plane to see anyone. One summer his parents asked him if he wanted to invite a friend to come and stay a week, and he invited me.

I was pretty excited. I got to fly on a plane by myself, the first time I'd ever done so, and I got to go to Germany, a country I'd never been to before. What was more, I'd be living on an Army base for a week, which sounded tremendously exciting to the kind of kid who had more than a little obsession with tanks and heavy artillery. On the down side, me and this kid weren't actually that close – we were in the same dorm, but we weren't exactly what my daughter would now call 'besties'.

While we might not have been close, I wasn't counting on me and this friend of mine falling out within hours of me getting there. However, that's exactly what happened. Looking back through the mists of time, I have absolutely no memory of why we fell out. I don't even remember the argument. What I do remember was feeling very much alone and far from home and this friend's Mum taking me aside and saying that she'd look after me, and maybe I might want to watch a video to take my mind off it. I can't imagine how delighted she was to have to entertain a child she didn't know who her son refused to speak to.

I liked watching films, but at that stage I didn't watch many of them what with school and all that, but I enjoyed them enough. My parents would occasionally get me to watch one with them, if I was interested enough to do so. But stuck there on an Army base with nobody to talk to, it made sense. I wouldn't need anyone to keep me company after all.

She set me up in the TV room with a bookcase full of videos. All black, no covers, just scrawled labels, pirated or taped off the telly, who knows. You have to assume that all the way out there in Germany there'd be a healthy trading scheme and tape-to-tape copying going on.

One of the tapes had one word on it – Aliens. I have no idea why I grabbed it, but grab it I did. If I grabbed any others, I don't recall them now. Only one.

Aliens.

I stuck it in the machine, probably as completely unaware of the age-inappropriateness as my friend's mother was of me grabbing such a grown up film. Down I sat, hoping for something to take my mind off my desperate and lonely situation.

Two hours later, terrified and thrilled and transported to another world, I rewound the tape and hit play again. And again.

And again. I loved it, was fascinated by it. Repelled and drawn in and absolutely captivated by it.

In the days that remained of my trip, I didn't make up with my now-ex friend (we would never reconcile) but I did rewatch that VHS, again and again and again. Having never seen Alien parts of it didn't make any sense, and as a kid other elements were just as strange to me, but I was drawn in by it. I don't know how many times I watched it, but it was enough that by the time I climbed the steps to get back on a plane (much to the relief of all involved, I'm sure) I knew every beat, every line, every jump.

I returned to England utterly enthused for this strange world. The first VHS I asked my parents to buy was Alien (I think they managed to hold out a little while) and the first comics I ever bought were Alien vs Predator. I bought the Allen Dean Foster tie-in novelisations, and as soon as the director's Cut came out, I was on that, too. In short, I got obsessed in the way only kids can. Soon I branched out to other films, discovering the twin joys of Horror and Action movies, and developing a penchant for anything with Tom Cruise in it.

And now, as a man in his forties putting the finishing touches to the first season of this sci-fi horror serial set on a strange land with mysterious creatures, I wonder what might have come of me if I hadn't fallen out with the kid from school whose name I barely recall?

One thing is for sure, I reckon Wyn wouldn't be having such a tough time on that ice moon...

I really hope you've enjoyed the first season of The Sunset Chronicles. If you have, I'd really appreciate if you could take a few moments to go back and leave a quick review (or even just stars) on the five episodes. This helps me get the series into more hands, and is honestly the best thing in the world.

See you again in Season Two,

Thanks,

Paul

GOT BLOOD?

An apocalyptic storm. A killer on the loose.
The battle for humanity's survival starts here.

About the Author

Paul Stephenson writes pulp fiction for the digital age. His first novel series – the apocalyptic *Blood on the Motorway* trilogy – has been an Amazon bestseller on both sides of the Atlantic. A former journalist, he has a diploma in Creative Writing from Oxford University.

His stories have been featured on the chart-topping horror podcasts, *The Other Stories* and *The Night's End*. His newest project, the ebook serial *The Sunset Chronicles*, is a dystopian sci-fi thriller that will delight and terrify fans of science fiction and horror alike. He is also the creator of the podcast *Bleakwood*, tales of terror from a mysterious English town, and one half of the *All Creatives Now* team, with fellow horror author, Kev Harrison.

He lives in England with his wife, two children, and one hell-hound.

To keep up to date with his books, please visit his website PaulStephensonBooks.com

Also by Paul Stephenson

DARKNESS RISES

When darkness comes, it doesn't ask permission. Get Darkness Come Alive, the first book in the new vampire epic from the author of Blood on the Motorway and the Sunset Chronicles.

BLOOD ON THE MOTORWAY

Blood on the Motorway
An apocalyptic storm. A killer on the loose. The battle for humanity's survival starts here.
Sleepwalk City

The fight for control has begun. Who will prevail in the battle for humanity's future in the pulse-quickening sequel to Blood on the Motorway?

A Final Storm

The sky is full of lights once more, and the survivors will need more than luck to get them through the coming storm. Who will survive, and who will thrive, in this heart-pounding finale to the Blood on the Motorway saga?

SUNSET CHRONICLES

Plague. Murder. Unrest. Humanity's future looks far from bright.

The year is 2107, and Earth is dying. For Wyn, Lois, and Judd, that's the least of their problems. Each holds a key to Earth's cure and humanity's survival in The Sunset Chronicles, the new sci-fi horror thrill-ride from Paul Stephenson, author of the bestselling British horror saga, Blood on the Motorway.

BLEAKWOOD

Introducing Bleakwood, a horror podcast from the creator of Blood on the Motorway and the Sunset Chronicles.

In the years since the fall, many of us have tried to find out why. To find what lead us here. But with so much of the old world gone, there are more questions than answers. What tore a hole in the world? Can we ever get it back?

But I think I've found something. A binder in the rubble. Don't ask me where. Full of stories about a little town called Bleakwood, stories that seem to show a way that....

They're not in any order, really. And I might be wrong. They might not have the answer. But I think it's in here.

A way back. To the before.

Listen, I'm just going to read them out, and you judge for yourself.

DARE YOU VENTURE INTO BLEAKWOOD?

WHAT TORE A HOLE IN THE WORLD?
CAN WE EVER GET IT BACK?

Find out in Bleakwood, the new horror podcast from the creator of Blood on the Motorway and The Sunset Chronicles

Created and narrated by Paul Stephenson and with stories by some of the most exciting voices in British modern Horror, subscribe to Bleakwood for a fresh story every month.

SCAN ME